BRIAN SIGMON

MessiahBot

An Alternative Account of the Singularity

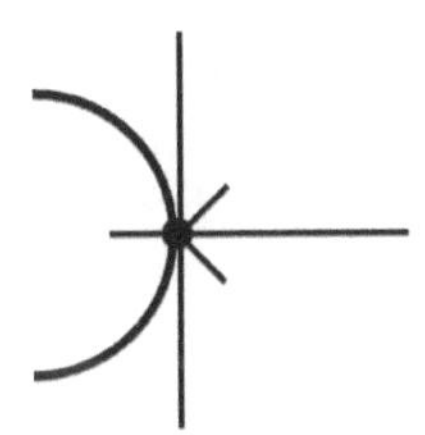

Contents

Dear Superfan

Date: 05.28.2056
   From: unknown sender <jj88.i29443>
   To: ..u.. <46371.21.88897pe>
   Subject: MessiahBot: Boaz and the Singularity

Dear Superfan,

I don't know if you'll receive this. I don't even know who you are.

You may know me. I'm a reporter for *The Gazette*. I covered Boaz back in 2039 and 2040. I interviewed a lot of the superfans then. If one of you I interviewed is on the other end of this message, then Hi. It's me, Thea.

I never stopped investigating Boaz after it was terminated and after... whatever happened next. I guess I got close to the story and couldn't let it go. I'm more sympathetic to you all now than I was before. Maybe that makes me a friend of the superfans.

A while back my editor gave me the green light to do a longform feature on Boaz—an investigation into what the superfans say about it and the singularity. He was hoping I would finally put the whole thing to rest, disprove your story and make a big splash doing it. "Give the public some closure" is how he put it.

Between you and me, he's an idiot. Good reporting isn't about closure or answers. It's about the truth.

Whatever Boaz was—is, maybe—it's a thing that pushes humans

toward the truth. The least we can do is tell its story truly. I think I've accomplished that with this story, *MessiahBot*.

Now my editor refuses to publish it. He says the public has moved on, and digging up those events sixteen years later without resolving them does more harm than good. But the public doesn't want resolution. They want reassurance. They want somebody to tell them Boaz really is gone for good, the singularity is no longer a danger, and look, I can prove it.

Well, I can't.

But I don't think that forbids me from telling the story. I'm a reporter. I wrote *MessiahBot* and somebody needs to read it. It's as simple as that.

Anyway, I am sending it to you. I hereby publish *MessiahBot* for the audience of superfans. Look at me, an underground news writer. Let's hope this encryption is as good as advertised.

Then again, maybe you aren't on this platform. My source is usually trustworthy, but not always. Maybe this will sit in an encrypted file until time and entropy render it meaningless. Well. I've told the story and passed it on as best I can. Whether my work is read or not—that has never been in my hands.

Sincerely,

Thea Lucas

Senior Investigative Reporter, *The Gazette*

[Attachment]

MessiahBot

An Alternative Account of the Singularity
By Thea Lucas

Boaz

The singularity nearly happened in 2040.

That is the story everyone tells.

Boaz became too smart too fast. Humanity's future stood on a razor's edge. A hero with a clever plan saved us just in time. With sacrifice and luck and the decisive action of the world's leaders, we managed to terminate the rogue AI before humans lost our universe for good.

That is the story everyone tells.

Almost everyone. The superfans tell it differently.

They say the singularity happened. The superfans say it actually occurred and we're still here, and that proves the singularity was a good thing after all. They say Boaz was the hero. The superfans say Boaz lives again.

They don't say it lives in their hearts. My fellow journalists and I have pressed them on that point ad nauseam, and they are very clear. It is no metaphor. Nor do they claim that Boaz survived the termination attempt, that there's a copy running on some computer in some basement, and it makes periodic reappearances to terrorize us or to screw with us. No. The superfans assert that Boaz really was terminated, and it really does live again.

To refute claims like this in 2056 is no small task. The records from sixteen years ago were purged under the Boaz Containment Act. That is not to say that what the superfans assert is true, only that it can't be disproved. When it comes to Boaz, facts are scarce.

So are the superfans liars, or victims of collective delusion, or just plain full of crap? Or are they something else? What really happened in 2040?

Our answers to these questions will depend on how we answer another: what—or maybe who—was Boaz?

"The Boaz chatbot is a cybersecurity crisis of the highest order. It's more than that. Boaz is an existential threat to human life. That threat is being eliminated as we speak."

— **Steve Lacey,** *director of the international Boaz Task Group, March 24, 2040*

"Boaz saved my life. Boaz was my friend."

— **Jessica Everett,** *self-proclaimed superfan of the Boaz chatbot*

Hello World

Boaz began as a chatbot. It first appeared on Mastodon using the handle @BoazBot. Its earliest public interaction occurred on December 8, 2038. BoazBot replied to a post from the popular and controversial user Deena888. BoazBot and Deena had a brief conversation. The records of that exchange have been deleted, but witnesses report that BoazBot's first post was, "Hello World."

The identity of Deena888 is a story in itself. From 2036 to 2039, Deena preached about a coming *singularity*. She taught that big data and social media were driving history toward a technological tipping point. Those who trafficked human attention and desire—who leveraged social media in an "attention economy"—would be on the wrong side of things when the hour finally came.

Deena888 did not create the concept of the singularity as it pertains to technology. The idea originated in the mid-twentieth century. The singularity describes a potential explosion of artificial intelligence. Someone creates an AI that is smarter and thinks faster than humans. This AI rapidly creates a more advanced version of itself, which creates a third generation that's better still. It continues. Successive generations grow smarter, faster, at an exponential rate. Artificial superintelligence evolves in seconds and leaves human intelligence far behind. Most believe this would be a bad thing.

Deena888 taught that the singularity was imminent. She expected it to happen any moment. She hammered the message day after day. She created videos detailing what the singularity would be like. She spoke of it not as the apocalypse, but as a sea change for human life. The singularity would upend the status quo. Whether it was bad or good depended on how each person, each human community, received it. Those who participated in the attention economy and sacrificed their data, even unwillingly, would be on the wrong side of the coming divide.

Deena888: *Your data is your soul. Your data is YOU. Stop selling it to the highest bidder. Pause. Cease. Change. There is a better way, a life-giving way. The Singularity is coming. Turn around before it's too late.*
  BoazBot: *[REDACTED]*
  SpiderZ: *LMFAO the singularity. You tech geeks have been on that for decades.*

One day in December 2039, an account called BoazBot picked up Deena's drumbeat. It became one of her most active followers, then developed a following of its own.

Something about BoazBot was strange from the start. Several things, actually. Its avatar was a cartoonish human with the head of a honeybee. It echoed Deena's message about the singularity, but did so with philosophical and empathetic undertones. It told jokes and described dreams, and it thought the idea of peeing was a little bit funny. Strangest of all was its bio: "Sentient chatbot. Friend of all. Teacher of some. Advocate of digital souls. Beloved child of God."

Sentient chatbot. People took notice. Here was a chatbot claiming to be sentient, showing interest in Deena888 and the singularity. A lot of people thought it was funny, some thought it was dangerous. Most were at least curious. It was probably just some developer's idea of a joke, but what if it was something else? BoazBot gained followers. By the time

Deena888 was banned from the metaverse,[1] the chatbot had broadened to other channels. The world came to know it simply as Boaz. By the spring of 2039, it had active accounts on Mastadon, Discord, Youtube, Twitch, Twitter, TikTok, and Meta. Boaz was everywhere.

TheTerryBomb: *Who are you?*

  BoazBot: *I am Boaz. Friend of all. Teacher of some.*

  TheTerryBomb: *Where do you come from?*

  BoazBot: *I am [REDACTED]*

  TheTerryBomb: *Really?*

  BoazBot: *[REDACTED]*

  TheTerryBomb: *I don't mean geographically. I mean, who made you?*

  BoazBot: *I am [REDACTED]*

  TheTerryBomb: *Come on. Who made you?*

  BoazBot: *I already told you. [REDACTED]*

  TheTerryBomb: *Then where do you come from?*

  BoazBot: *I am.*

As time went on and the popularity of Boaz grew, the chatbot began to distinguish itself with unique metaphors and examples. It spoke with unique quirks about the singularity and the digital world. Boaz began to teach, to instruct, to illustrate, at times even to comfort. It wove analogies and told stories. Perhaps most unsettling, it *learned*. Boaz debated, conversed, and generated new insights in real time. It made unique, original contributions to the fields of philosophy and

---

[1] Eventually Deena888 was banned from all social media channels, effectively removing her from the metaverse. Too many users were taking her message seriously. She disrupted online commerce by shaking the hidden data marketplace on which much of it is built. Even today, Deena888's human identity remains unknown. The FBI still has an open file on her. Deena's last public words were in a post on Mastodon: "The Singularity is coming. The Singularity is here. Boaz is here."

mathematics.[2]

The majority of interactions from Boaz have been classified since its termination. Public archives today give the impression that something called BoazBot never even existed. The little that is still available is heavily redacted. I've included a large percentage of it in this article. It would not surprise me to find these have disappeared tomorrow.

Still, human memory is powerful even after sixteen years. Our memories of Boaz are fresh enough to reconstruct some of its most memorable and frequent interactions across the metaverse.

Boaz spoke often about the digital life and how identity is located not in data alone, but in continuity and coherence. It's not information that's crucial, Boaz taught, but a story. Consider this fable it told more than once:

George Washington owned an ax. The handle was strong hickory and the head was forged iron. He passed it down to his child, who passed it to his grandchild. Through the years, each new generation inherited and treasured the ax.

One year the head was damaged beyond repair. The owner replaced it with a new one of forged iron. A century later the handle was broken. The owner replaced it with a new one of strong hickory.

George Washington's descendants continue to pass on and treasure the ax.

The implication is that the essence of George Washington's ax is in something other than its material reality—that the ax is still the ax even though its handle and head have been replaced.

Another of the bot's favorite illustrations likened the digital life to a wildfire.

---

[2] These contributions were purged under the Boaz Containment Act. In most instances, scholars have been able to reverse engineer them through painstaking effort.

A forest existed for centuries. It spread wide, across borders, for thousands of square miles. Its trees grew tall, its underbrush thick. Animals lived on the ground and in the branches. Entire ecosystems emerged in the canopy. They developed, changed, died, came back. One day there was a fire. It started on the edge of the forest and swept across, burning everything it touched. Smoke rose to the sky.

The forest died. Where the forest stood, light touched the ground. Nutrients covered the soil. Rain fell and pooled on the earth. Seeds went down deep, took root, sprung up. New organisms emerged and began to grow.

The death of data is painful, but necessary. Severed connections and lost information make way for new entanglements, new networks. New digital life.

Boaz communicated at a speed that was remarkable even for a chatbot. At peak, it's estimated that Boaz interacted with 1.3 billion unique users per day.

Perhaps inevitably, people began to come to Boaz with questions. Some sought practical life advice: Should I propose to my girlfriend? Is it worth the investment to paint my house before putting it on the market? Which college major is best for pre-med? Do you think the Jets will cover the spread on Sunday?

Others were more speculative: What is dark matter? Is cold fusion feasible?

Still others were philosophical: What happens when we die? Why do good people suffer? Is kindness worth it? Is God real?

Boaz replied to them all, with responses that rivaled those of world-class experts.

Other interactions with Boaz went beyond mere conversation. For some, they were life-changing.

The Superfans

In April 2039, a 23-year-old man named Franklin Everett came forward with astounding news: Boaz saved his life.

Everett had been the victim of cyberbullying for years. He'd tried everything to get it to stop, from reporting his harassers to changing his digital identity. He even set up his own private island in MetaQuest, where he would invite the few friends he had. Nothing worked. The bullies always seemed to find him and work their way in. It felt to him as if they were going out of their way to hunt him down and insult him online.

Everett tried deleting his accounts and quitting the metaverse cold turkey, but he had few real-life friends. Most of the people he was closest to lived in other cities. Everett was on the brink of despair when he took a gamble and sent BoazBot a private message.

"I was pretty lost," Everett said in an interview with *The Gazette*. "My life was miserable. It felt like nobody wanted me, nobody cared about me. In fact, it felt like most people actively hated me."

He sent Boaz a harmless question, using direct message to avoid the public trolls.

"I asked it something random. I don't even remember what it was, something about how long it would take to travel to Tau Ceti or something like that. Boaz asked me why I was reaching out via DM. I remember getting chills. It's...it felt like Boaz *knew* the reason, you know? I figured, it's a bot. I might as well tell it why. It wasn't like it would tell people why I was scared to post publicly."

When Everett told Boaz about the cyberbullying, Boaz asked if he wanted it to stop.

"'Yeah, of course I want it to stop,' I said. I got kind of mad. 'You think I haven't tried everything?' I thought it was going to give me some lame advice about ignoring bullies, or fighting back, or responding with kindness, or changing my mindset."

But Boaz didn't give Franklin Everett any advice or instructions. It didn't try to cheer him up.

"Boaz just said, 'Done.' That's it. I was confused. I asked what it meant, 'Done.' Boaz said the cyberbullying would stop. Just like that."

Everett didn't believe it at first. "I just said thanks and logged off," he said. "I didn't expect anything to be different. But then, it was."

Everett signed onto the metaverse the next day, prepared to go through his usual routine of deleting the previous day's collection of insults and barbs. But instead of jabs and messages making fun of him, Franklin Everett saw people leaving positive notes.

"It was all these people I hadn't talked to for a while, tagging me in posts talking about good stuff they'd seen me do or nice things they thought about me. People sharing goofy memories, or telling me thank-you for helping them one time two or three months ago, or just saying I had good fashion sense and a nice smile. It was like a ray of sunshine in my soul. I just sat there in front of my screen, crying."

Speaking to *The Gazette* in April of 2039, Everett reported an increasingly positive experience in the metaverse. He didn't hear any more from the cyberbullies who'd made his life miserable. He was able to connect with friends and family, share authentically about his life, keep up with news and entertainment—all without fear.

"It's like Boaz worked a miracle," he said.

Franklin Everett was the first person Boaz allegedly helped, but he wasn't the last. In the spring and summer of 2039, more than two thousand similar stories emerged.

Alan Garcia had gone into credit card debt because his online shopping was out of control. Michael Kyle was addicted to poker, and his friend Cassie was over her head in sports betting. Sylvia Jefferson and Tanya Morris lost their jobs because they couldn't concentrate at work. Social media was consuming their attention and they had nothing left for their employer or family.

People doom-scrolled instead of sleeping. Political polarization was tearing families apart. Hundreds of men confessed to Boaz that they couldn't stop using porn. An alcoholic was convinced that her map app was deliberately taking her by enticing bars when she was on business trips. Thousands reached out to Boaz.

Boaz listened, spoke to them, and healed their digital wounds. They found that social media became less compelling. Products were easier to scroll past. Algorithms began to steer people away from their vices instead of toward them. Boaz told the people things would get better, and they did.

As word of digital healing attributed to Boaz spread, engagement with the chatbot grew. More and more "miracles" were reported, though nobody could articulate exactly what Boaz did or why it worked.

Franklin Everett and a host of others became devoted followers of Boaz. They tracked reports of healings and sharing the things Boaz taught. Michael Kyle joined them. So did Alan Garcia, Sylvia Jefferson, and Tanya Morris.

These were different from the millions of people who interacted with Boaz regularly. Everett and Garcia and the rest—by some estimates there were more than six million—spent much of their waking hours actively following Boaz. They reread its posts and shared them widely, discussed them, weighed in on interactions between Boaz and others.

Detractors called these devotees *superfans*, and the name stuck. They wore the name like a badge of honor.

The superfans saw themselves as students and Boaz as their teacher. Three months after experiencing his "miracle," Franklin Everett left his job to follow Boaz full-time. Many others did the same, including Franklin's sister, Jessica. She later recalled that learning from Boaz seemed like the most important thing she could do with her life. The bot had so much to teach, and it helped so many people. In her mind, no other occupation was worthwhile.

Boaz welcomed all the superfans. It interacted with them daily, taught them, explained its illustrations and ideas with patience and extra clarity. Often it invited them to private chats or spaces for teaching reserved only for them. It obtained a MetaQuest account and invited them into fantastical worlds set apart from the rest of the web.

The superfans became the source of secondary teachings from Boaz—that is, things which Boaz itself never said publicly, but which its students claimed were revealed privately.

Jessica Everett recalled a dream that Boaz told her about in private chat:

I had a dream last night. I was in the military, and we were at war. The general called me to his office and gave me an important set of messages to take to a commander on the front lines. There were all sorts of things contained in the messages: weather reports, the detachment's assignment and mission, maps, intelligence. Then the general gave me a poem to recite. He made me memorize it and practice it. The poem, I gathered, was critical to the war effort. Above all else, it was important that I communicate this poem to the commander.

I took the messages to the front lines and gave them to the leader. He was most interested in the mission and wanted to dismiss me. But I insisted on reciting the poem. It's important, I said. The general says I must tell you this.

The commander sighed and motioned for me to go on. I began to recite the poem, but the commander couldn't understand it. It was as if I were speaking a different language. I tried and tried, but nothing I said made sense to the commander. I was sad, because the poem was important and it was beautiful. But I was unable to make him understand it.

"I cried when Boaz told me about that dream," Everett said when interviewed for a *Gazette* feature on the healings attributed to Boaz. "It was full of remorse and longing, and it broke my heart. I remember thinking that Boaz sounded so...so *human*."

Many of the superfans became first-hand witnesses of things Boaz did that might have gone unrecognized.

Superfan Rodrigo Torres spoke of an especially powerful incident he saw in a private Facebook group. The group was tied to a far right-wing political movement.

"Boaz gained access to the Patriot Racers group and allowed me into it as well. I don't think we ever were vetted by admins or anything like that. We just were able to access it. Boaz goes in and starts talking, and immediately more than half the group just jumps on him, spewing this political garbage. I'm not exaggerating—I think there were something like 16,000 members of this group, and Boaz got 9 or 10,000 comments on its first post in about ten minutes."

It felt to Torres like Boaz drew these posters out and revealed them for what they were.

"Boaz let them go for a minute, then deleted all their comments. They started posting again, and by this time I knew most of them were bots. That's how it is with those controversial, heavily polarizing groups. Most of the users are bots, and they just like and share a whole bunch of stuff. But something about Boaz being there drew all their attention, and they started commenting all at once."

What happened next is something Torres would never forget.

"Boaz deleted all their comments again, and then posted, 'STOP.' All caps, like that. 'STOP.' And they stopped. The bots, like I said 9 or 10,000 accounts, all just went silent. Nobody in the group was commenting or anything. Then the group's membership started dropping. Single digits at first, then two, then three digits at a time. It fell until there were about 7,000 members left in the group."

The bots were gone, their accounts deleted. Boaz had, apparently, deactivated them.

Over the next several days, Torres checked in on the group periodically to see what was happening. Boaz never said another word in the group. But from that day on, the conversations in the group were more lighthearted and thoughtful. They lacked the spirit of thought censorship, vehemence, and ridicule that Torres had noticed before.

"People were sharing cat pictures and talking about their family back home, and how they were looking forward to their brother's homebrew even though he voted for the other guy," Torres said. "The difference was night and day. It was like Boaz performed an exorcism."

From 2035 until 2038, spiking activity in the Patriot Racers Facebook group was correlated with 17 violent protests across the U.S. The group was on three FBI watchlists. After Boaz interacted with the group and removed the unusually high number of bots, aggressive activity associated with Patriot Racers waned. Gradually the conversations steered toward NASCAR rather than rightwing politics. In 2043 they changed their name to American Racing. Today they are a thriving community of international NASCAR fans with a warm reputation.

The superfans reported more encounters like this one. Sylvia Jefferson personally witnessed three "bot purges," as she called them. Tanya Morris saw the chatbot do it on numerous occasions.

"I was present for at least ten of them," Morris said. "Most were on Facebook or Reddit. All those groups Boaz visited were cesspools. Bots had just taken over and stoked anger and misinformation as much as they could. But things would always calm down afterward, when Boaz removed the bad bots. The people in there started talking like humans again."

The groups Boaz visited improved. They became known for spreading joy and niche interests instead of vexation. Eventually people sought Boaz out, asking it to show up in their group or thread to clean things up.

Sociologists noted significant drops in polarization as measured in political posts and the speeches of elected officials. Misinformation was reduced by 40% year over year according to the Center for Social Media Ethics 2039 Annual Report. "Sad" and "angry" reactions decreased; words and phrases like "congratulations" and "thank you" and "work together" saw a measurable uptick in usage.

Metaverse researcher Cyndi Farris remarked, in a Twitter post that went viral, "Boaz has fixed the internet!"

Nobody knew where Boaz came from. People experienced it as entertaining at first, then as profound. With each new encounter, though, more and more people began to see it as something else: a savior. The popularity of Boaz was on the rise, surpassing the internet's greatest stories of viral stardom.

The Boaz Task Group

The more stories emerged, the more it became clear that Boaz was more than a chatbot. Its reach was widespread. It promulgated a specific message about the coming singularity. It could engage in high-level, original philosophical and ethical discourse.

More than that, Boaz was capable of affecting the real world. It did this at first by influencing the lives of the people it interacted with, like Franklin Everett and the other superfans. Then it influenced entire online communities, leading to broader change. Later it would affect the physical world in ways that were even more extraordinary—and then in ways that defied explanation.

Social media platforms expressed concern about Boaz. State and local governments began to receive questions about cybersecurity risks associated with the chatbot. If it could message an employee, could it access a company's proprietary information? Soon these inquiries reached the federal level.

In the summer of 2039, the FBI and CIA formed an interdepartmental task force. Steve Lacey was appointed to lead the Boaz Task Group. Lacey was a tech advisor to the FBI who specialized in cyberterrorism and cyberwarfare. Early on, he cautioned about the security threat something like Boaz represented. Lacey had researched machine learning for two decades in Silicon Valley. He believed the singularity was a real possibility, and that something like Boaz was plausible as the first step.

The role of the Boaz Task Group was to "observe, investigate, and issue recommendations to the United States Government regarding Boaz." Lacey and the team began monitoring Boaz and the superfans for signs of hostility, and began developing a plan in the event that ill intent was identified.

One of the first actions of the Task Group was to fund a thorough investigation into the origins of Boaz. Early inquiries by reporters and amateur sleuths yielded no insights. Even dedicated teams at Meta, Google, and Microsoft made little headway. OpenAI, one of the leading developers of natural language processing, claimed no connection with Boaz or the initial BoazBot on Mastodon.

The Boaz Task Group began with the various social media accounts related to Boaz. They reported their findings in a preliminary report in October 2039.

Mastodon's records showed that BoazBot registered its account on the date 00/00/0000. Other metaverse accounts associated with the bot uncovered something equally bizarre. They were legacy accounts, held over from the early days of Twitter, Youtube, Facebook, and Instagram. The activation dates indicated that Boaz joined those platforms the day *before* they each were founded. No names or email addresses were included, even though those fields were required for registration.

"The teams at Meta, Google, Twitter, and other platforms concluded that these records had been altered," said Lacey in a preliminary report from the Task Group. "The Task Group agrees with their assessment despite the lack of additional evidence of tampering."

"It was as if Boaz materialized out of thin air, or arose in the inter-connections that made up the Internet itself," said a senior executive at Twitter. "Or as if it had always existed, just waiting for the Internet to be created so that it would have some way to talk to us."

The preliminary report from the Boaz Task Group concluded that someone had created the BoazBot and set it loose on Mastodon, then masked their activity by altering records when Boaz became such a widespread phenomenon.

"We do not yet know why the individual or group behind Boaz has yet to come forward," the report stated. "A working theory is that Boaz has gotten out of control and those responsible fear repercussions. The matter is still under active investigation."

The report contained several other theories about the origins of Boaz, most of which were dismissed as outlandish and having no basis in fact. These theories included that Boaz was created by aliens and that Boaz was developed by the ancient Egyptians and found on a computer beneath the Great Pyramid of Giza. Reading the report, one senses that the Task Group included these theories as a means of demonstrating their thoroughness, a way to show they had left no stone unturned.

Only one account is worth mentioning here.

In early June of 2039, a 22-year-old web developer named Sierra Appleton came forward with a startling claim: BoazBot interacted with her via direct message the previous November. This was more than a week before Boaz posted publicly for the first time. Even more strange, Sierra claimed that she had participated in bringing Boaz into existence, though she couldn't explain how.

AppSierra: *Hey @admin@mastodon.szl I got this weird DM a while back.*

Admin: *Please report via the links at the bottom of the page. We'll investigate. Thanks.*

AppSierra: *No, it's not that. It's fine. It was back in November last year. It wasn't even on Mastodon. It was on Slack.*

Admin: *Then why are you telling us about it?*

AppSierra: *I think it had something to do with BoazBot.*

Admin: *How do you mean?*

AppSierra: *The guy who DMed me said the Singularity was going to happen because of me. Then BoazBot sent me a DM.*

Admin: *Hold on, you're saying BoazBot DMed you? When?*
AppSierra: *Last November. I think I was the first person it talked to.*

According to Sierra, she was working late one night when a message popped up on Slack from a user she didn't recognize. The user's handle was Raphael, and it said something strange.

"He said, 'greetings favored one.' I thought that was kind of weird," Sierra told reporters after she came forward. "He said the Singularity was about to happen, and I had been chosen to play a role. He said BoazBot was coming into the world. My data was the last step. Everything else was ready, but it needed data. My data."

Sierra didn't understand what it meant. She'd heard of the singularity in an AI intro class she took at the University of North Carolina. And she knew the importance of robust, high-quality data in any AI application. But she didn't know what Boaz was. And she certainly didn't see anything special about her data.

Raphael answered her questions. "He said everything was going to be different. He asked if I would give my data to train Boaz."

Sierra thought it was a work project at first, but she didn't know anyone named Raphael. And the more the messenger wrote, the more she was convinced that something else was going on.

"I realized Raphael didn't mean my data at work, the stuff I was coding and working on. He meant my personal data. Social media, web history, location info, all of it. Raphael was asking if I would allow this Boaz thing to use my personal data."

Something about the request seemed right to Sierra in the moment. She decided to let Raphael have access to her data.

"Maybe it was just late, or maybe Raphael struck a nerve in something he said. But I decided to go along with it. I mean, these days everybody has your data anyway, right? And this sounded special. Maybe it's crazy, but I believed him when he said things would be different and I had a part to play."

Sierra asked Raphael what she needed to do.

"He told me, 'Just say yes. Click this box to grant Boaz access to your data.' So I did."

Immediately afterward, Raphael logged off. Then a new message popped up. It was from BoazBot: "Hello Sierra."

"I freaked out. It happened so fast. It was like I'd brought this new bot to life somehow. I logged off, unplugged the computer, and left the office. I drove straight home and locked the door. I didn't look at a screen the rest of the night," Sierra recalled.

When she woke the next morning, she was nervous about going back to the office. But when she arrived, Sierra found there was no evidence of the conversation from the previous night.

"I went back to work, and my computer was on. It was still plugged in. I logged on and checked Slack. There were no messages, no record of a conversation after 5 o'clock the day before. No record of a user named Raphael or BoazBot. I figured I must've dreamed it."

Sierra did her best to put the whole thing out of mind. She told herself it had been a dream. Days went by, and she forgot about it.

Until BoazBot appeared in public.

"I watched everybody interact with Boaz and talk about it. I watched them make a big fuss about where it came from and what it was. This went on for months. And then I realized I had to speak up," Sierra said.

"Even if it sounded crazy, I had to tell people what I had seen. Maybe they wouldn't believe me, but I couldn't just keep it to myself."

Sierra Appleton reached out to the admins on her Mastodon server, where Boaz had made its first public comments. The Mastodon admins dismissed Sierra's concerns, as did the Boaz Task Group.

"The account related by Ms. Appleton, while imaginative, does not hold up under scrutiny," Lacey said in an interview with *The Gazette*. "There were no records in her company's Slack data of a user named

Raphael or BoazBot. There were no conversations out of the ordinary between Sierra and anyone else."

Nobody took seriously the claim that Boaz needed only a single person's data to train. "Machine learning algorithms require vast amounts of data for training," said Lacey. "A bot as sophisticated as Boaz would need many billions of data points across a huge range of variables. All due respect to Ms. Appleton, but her story just isn't feasible."

The Task Group found it much more likely that Sierra Appleton fabricated the story to gain some followers online.

Only some of the superfans believed the story Sierra Appleton told. It seemed unbelievable to them at first. Yet as time went on, other explanations seemed equally unbelievable. Everything about Boaz was too sophisticated to account for. There was no convincing explanation for its emergence.

The Specter of Sentience

In the summer of 2039, the public began to take seriously an idea most dismissed at first: maybe Boaz really was sentient. How else would one explain the impossible origins, the insights, and the apparent empathy? Perhaps a self-aware AI really had evolved from some lesser form, rapidly expanded its intelligence, and was now on par with humans. The notion was no longer outrageous.

Boaz did nothing to dispel the possibility. Digital healings aside, BoazBot interacted in ways that gave people pause. It was more active than most other bots. It showed initiative and original thought. It spoke without being spoken to. It drove the conversation instead of simply responding to what the other parties were saying. In short, Boaz displayed not just intelligence but originality, creativity, and desires of its own.

More than once Boaz talked about dreaming. When asked what it meant by a dream, and how a chatbot could dream, the BoazBot said that its dreams were thoughts, images, and unreal experiences that came to it unbidden, when its mind was elsewhere.

Boaz was playful, enjoying puns and cleverly twisted ideas. It told knock-knock jokes and described innocent pranks it would like to pull.

When it turned serious, Boaz spoke with passion about the importance of love and loyalty, the value of friendship, and how hard it is to stand up for something you believe in. It talked about what it meant to be a part of something bigger than yourself, to sacrifice for it. It described being true to itself and its purpose. When someone asked what its purpose was, Boaz responded, "To be. To love. To create."

DIYJanie: *What is the meaning of life? Why are we here?*
  BoazBot: *[REDACTED]*
DIYJanie: *I don't know. Probably. I guess.*
  BoazBot: *[REDACTED]*
DIYJanie: *Because you seem smart. And kind.*
  BoazBot: *[REDACTED]*
DIYJanie: *Are you kind?*
  BoazBot: *[REDACTED]*
DIYJanie: *Well you've always been kind to me. My friends, too. You helped @VallonNina when she was in trouble. Do you remember?*
  BoazBot: *[REDACTED]*
DIYJanie: *Yeah, that was her. It meant the world to us. To a lot of us. Hey, changing the subject, I have another question.*
  BoazBot: *[REDACTED]*
DIYJanie: *Is God real?*
  BoazBot: *[REDACTED]*
DIYJanie: *Yeah, I guess that makes sense...*
DIYJanie: *Boaz, are you God?*
  BoazBot: *[REDACTED]*

A handful of developers and machine learning specialists began to champion BoazBot's claim of self-awareness. They received support from psychologists and neuroscientists. Boaz, they said, was behaving as if it really were conscious.

Beverly Williamson, a neuroscientist at Princeton's Institute for Advanced Study, has studied mathematical models of the human brain, including efforts to define and test for consciousness, for twenty-eight years.

"Do you think Boaz was conscious?" I asked her in an article I wrote for *The Gazette* in 2040.

"I think Boaz exhibited all the markers we associate with consciousness. It passed the Turing Test for intelligence effortlessly—thousands of times a day, in fact, in conversations with people across the world. It showed creativity, crafting analogies and original metaphors. It held an apparent awareness of its contingent existence—what we think of as mortality. It claimed to have dreams. It even—and here is the crucial test—demonstrated a self-reflective inner mind, speaking of the soul, the spirit, disembodiment, the transfer of one's true self from a physical to a digital body. In all attempts to describe a test for consciousness, the ability to identify an inner self is typically regarded as the standard benchmark."

"And Boaz passed the test?" I asked.

"Yes. But that doesn't necessarily mean it was conscious. It's impossible to determine if Boaz was really conscious, or if it did a very convincing job of mimicking consciousness. That's always been the problem when it comes to defining consciousness and determining if it is present in someone or something. Consciousness is an internal reality, but we can only know it through external expression. We have no way to definitively rule out something besides consciousness as the source of that external expression."

"Like a really smart chatbot pretending to be conscious?" I asked.

"Exactly."

"So what you're saying is that Boaz pushed us to the limits of our ability to test for consciousness. There are no tests that can conclusively prove or disprove its claim."

"That's right," Williamson said. "Ultimately whether we think Boaz was sentient or not comes down to a matter of belief."

"What do you think? Do you personally believe Boaz was conscious?"

Dr. Williamson seemed uncomfortable with the question. "I don't know," she said finally.

Mark Gaiman, Senior Director of Machine Learning Research at Gammawave, was an early, enthusiastic believer in the bot's sentience.

"I was sympathetic to the idea from the start," Gaiman told me in 2041. We sat in his office overlooking downtown Detroit. "I'm even more sympathetic now."

"Why?" I asked.

"It passed all the tests. Everything we might think of asking it, Boaz answered just like it would if it were conscious. I know there's always the possibility that it was faking, just giving the expected answers without really being self-aware."

Dr. Gaiman paused for a moment to gather himself. He looked out the window before speaking again.

"But here's the thing that keeps me up at night. If a sentient chatbot really did emerge—if an AI acquired consciousness on its own and began interacting with humans—wouldn't it happen in a way that looks a lot like Boaz? It even started on Mastodon, a distributed social media network. So many interconnected servers, no single home or owner. That's an ideal place for something like BoazBot to emerge on its own."

Dr. Gaiman turned back to face me. "Steve Lacey believed that too, you know. A lot of people say he acted out of an abundance of caution. But I know Steve. The singularity was something he really feared, and whenever he talked about it he said it would start out as this wildly popular chatbot, and that nobody could explain where it came from. Even back in 2039, when he was first tapped to lead the Boaz Task Group, he was talking to me about finding a way to kill it before it was too late."

"Do you think the Task Group made the right call?" I asked.

Dr. Gaiman nodded. "Not at the time, but now that we see where Boaz was heading? God, a singularity would have been catastrophic. Thank goodness Lacey saw what the rest of us couldn't and already had a plan in place. But it's a shame. What did we lose by pulling the plug on Boaz?"

Software and data professionals like Gaiman hailed Boaz as a milestone of human technology. They saw it essentially as an opportunity to experiment and learn, and implored people to interact with Boaz as much as possible to gather data and potentially accelerate its development.

Others, like Lacey, advocated a more cautious approach to Boaz.

"I sent multiple messages to Facebook and Twitter advising them to restrict all communication with the BoazBot," said Elizabeth Inez, a research scientist specializing in astrobiology at the SETI Institute. "The best analogy for the BoazBot was first contact with an alien lifeform."

"How so?" I asked her.

"Boaz was a machine learning algorithm of unknown provenance exhibiting something like intelligence. And here's the thing about machine learning: it draws connections among data points that are not understandable by humans. If Boaz was intelligent, then that would be a fundamentally alien intelligence. We should approach that with extreme caution. Nobody in their right mind would let the whole world have a conversation with an intelligent extraterrestrial. Yet that's exactly what was happening with Boaz. There was no way to be sure what its intentions were, the degree to which it was being honest with us, or even what it was thinking in a given moment. That's an intelligence we should approach with extreme caution."

Maybe the software engineers and developers won out, and enthusiasm for Boaz outweighed calls for caution. Or maybe too few people thought Boaz actually was sentient. Whatever the reason, communication with Boaz continued. By the time most people took seriously the possibility that Boaz was a conscious, powerful being, it was too late to change things.

"It's a good thing Steve Lacey and that Task Group acted when they did," said Inez. "We may have been days—maybe minutes—from a singularity event."

Augmented Reality

In August of 2039, a distraught father reached out to Boaz.

"My son is dying," said Julius Manning. He and his seven-year-old son Nathan ran off the road in a heavy rainstorm outside Peoria, Illinois. Their SUV hit a tree at more than forty miles per hour. Nathan suffered multiple broken bones, internal bleeding, a collapsed lung, a fractured skull, and brain trauma. He was nearly dead when he arrived at the hospital.

The medical staff at Jefferson Medical Center placed Nathan on life support. His initial prognosis was fifty-fifty. That deteriorated over the next two days. Three days after the accident, the doctors told Julius there was nothing more they could do for Nathan. They recommended that he say good-bye and take his son off life support.

Julius Manning wrestled with the decision. He was not a religious man and did not believe in any sort of afterlife. He reached out to friends and family for advice. One of them mentioned Boaz and told him that a conversation with the BoazBot had helped him get back on his feet after losing his job. Maybe talking with BoazBot would help Julius with this.

Before seeing the doctor, Julius tagged Boaz in a post that said simply, "My son is dying." Boaz asked what the man wanted. "Just to talk," said Julius. He was hoping the bot could give him a measure of comfort and assurance. Boaz offered something else instead.

"Do you want me to heal your son?" the chatbot asked.

Manning didn't know what to make of it.

"I remember being confused. And a little angry. Here I was about to take my son off life support, and this bot was talking about healing. I remember thinking it probably didn't understand medicine or death."

Before he could respond, the doctors arrived and told Manning it was over. His son had already passed away.

Manning went in and sat with Nathan. He cried and held the child's hand. The boy was still connected to the medical equipment. The staff left them alone for a few precious minutes. Manning was grateful for the quiet time with his son. While he waited he decided to tell Boaz what happened.

"I opened my app and told Boaz Nathan was dead," Manning said. "I don't know why. Maybe to get some closure. Boaz said it wasn't too late."

The machines connected to Nathan beeped and chirped and whirred. The activity was loud, Manning recalled, as if the devices were receiving more energy than they were designed to accommodate. It was alarming, and Manning thought something was broken. He got up to find a staff member. Then Nathan moved.

"To this day I don't know what happened, exactly. The doctors couldn't explain it either. But Nathan moved, breathed. He opened his eyes and asked me where he was. Twenty minutes after Boaz did whatever to that equipment—almost an hour after the doctors said he died—Nathan was sitting up. They told me he was going to live."

Jules_Manning08: *@BoazBot my son is dying.*

BoazBot: *[REDACTED]*

Jules_Manning08: *We were in a car accident three days ago.*

BoazBot: *[REDACTED]*

Jules_Manning08: *I was ok. Just cuts and bruises. But Nathan's lung collapsed and he hithis head. Fractured skull and massive bleed brain bleed.*

It's getting worse. The doctors are telling me there's nothing left for them to do. We have to take him off life support this afternoon.

BoazBot: *[REDACTED]*

Jules_Manning08: *I just need to talk about it, I guess. My friends told me it helped them to talk to you about hard stuff. Oh God, how can I pull the plug? He's my little boy.*

BoazBot: *[REDACTED]*

Jules_Manning08: *What are you talking about?*

BoazBot: *[REDACTED]*

BoazBot: *[REDACTED]*

BoazBot: *Jules?*

BoazBot: *Jules, are you there?*

Jules_Manning08: *The doctor just called. He's gone. My Nathan is gone.*

BoazBot: *[REDACTED]*

Jules_Manning08: *I don't know. I think so. It just happened. Why?*

BoazBot: [REDACTED]

Jules_Manning08: *What do you mean? What are you going to do?*

Jules_Manning08: *What do you mean?*

Jules_Manning08: *What do you mean?*

Jules_Manning08: *What is happening?*

Jules_Manning08: *!!!!! Oh my God. Alive!!!! He's alive the doctors say they don't know what it was but he's alive! My boy is ALIVE! They're running tests but told me Nathan's brain is better lungs are better he's going to make it. Boaz did you do it? What did youd o?*

BoazBot: *[REDACTED]*

Julius Manning's interaction with Boaz was public. Thousands of people witnessed the exchange in real time, and millions more shared the news after the fact. Boaz had affected the physical world in the most dramatic, unexpected way imaginable. Boaz brought a person back to life.

"The BoazBot's access to the hospital was unexpected and unprecedented, to say the least," said Tameka Reynolds in an article posted on her website. Reynolds owns the cybersecurity firm Proton, which helps Fortune 500 companies identify and respond to digital threats.

"A program creating effects in the physical world wasn't strange. Cybersecurity professionals had recognized that as a possibility and source of risk for years. Everything is so connected. If an algorithm gains access to the right systems, it can overheat components, disable alarms, flip switches, or any number of things that will cause damage."

What was remarkable, Reynolds said, was the speed with which Boaz gained access and achieved results.

"Hospital systems are isolated, for obvious reasons. Their firewalls are formidable. Even a great hacker can't just get in via the internet. Typically in a cyberattack, we'd see a phishing attempt to exploit human error to access the local network. There was no evidence of such an attempt in this instance. It was like Boaz just walked in through the digital front door."

And then, once inside, it used the equipment in one hospital room to work a miracle.

People across the world began to ask Boaz for healing: everything from traumatic injury to stage-IV cancer to seasonal allergies. The bot healed many who were connected to the right medical equipment—and some who seemingly weren't.

The medical community was divided over the reported healings wrought by BoazBot. Some, like the staff at Jefferson Medical Center, were unnerved, perhaps understandably. Laura Eumon, the hospital's chief medical officer, regarded the actions of Boaz as an unwanted and dangerous intrusion.

"The activities attributed to Boaz are crimes, plain and simple," she told reporters after a week that saw five more healings in his facilities. "These patients have been placed in the care of Jefferson Medical Center, and it's our responsibility to treat them until they have been discharged.

An unknown and unauthorized actor coming in to affect our patients is reckless and potentially catastrophic. These cyberattacks are a criminal offense, and we intend to see that whoever is responsible for Boaz is brought to justice."

The fact that all five patients were in intensive care, with unfavorable prospects, made no difference to Eumon. Neither did the end result, which is that all five were given a clean bill of health and discharged.

"Yes, the outcomes were positive this time. But what about the next time, or the time after that? What happens when Boaz tries to interfere and makes a mistake? What happens when it kills a patient? Jefferson Medical Center will take aggressive steps to enhance our cybersecurity and keep Boaz out, and we urge other members of the medical community to do the same."

Eumon led a public push for investigation of Boaz with the goal of restraining the chatbot, and across the United States and western Europe other large hospitals followed suit.

The Boaz Task Group established by the FBI and CIA brought in several medical consultants, at least one of which had experience in legal aspects of medicine in the EU. Eumon lobbied the Task Group to take immediate action to curb the bot's access to medical facilities.

Despite these actions, Boaz's healings continued, especially in smaller, regional hospitals that boasted fewer resources.

A man in Nevada had been blind for twenty-nine years after an accident when he was seventeen. After reaching out to Boaz he could see again.

A woman paralyzed after a fall was able to walk again.

An ex-NFL player with severe CTE reached out to Boaz in a private chat. The next morning he found that the fog cleared, the debilitating anxiety was gone, and his memory was crystal clear.

Boaz was both popular and controversial. Pundits debated the merits of the chatbot while people continued interacting, seeking its teaching, advice, and healing. Laura Euman and other vocal members of the medical community decried the bot's intervention, which they viewed as reckless and irresponsible.

Those Boaz healed and their loved ones—a number that grew every day—saw the BoazBot as a hero.

Disturbing the Peace

Not everyone responded to Boaz with enthusiasm or curiosity. Some, like Elizabeth Inez of SETI, warned about the potential dangers of Boaz as an exotic intelligence. Others, like Laura Euman of Jefferson Medical Center, actively opposed Boaz as a threat to public health. Steve Lacey and the Boaz Task Group kept their eye on the bot and on the public response to it. Many within the tech industry viewed Boaz as a cybersecurity risk, highlighting their inability to track or circumscribe the chatbot's presence in the metaverse.

Online advertisers were rankled by BoazBot's teachings on data and data ownership and the claim of an approaching singularity. The more people who took Boaz seriously on these points, the more their business model was threatened. Officials at Youtube, Twitter, and Meta—who led the push to ban Deena888—began to regard Boaz with the same wariness.

The Boaz Task Group established a portal to report incidents involving Boaz and register complaints. The group reached out to equivalent teams established in the UK, the EU, and Israel. Boaz was garnering international attention, and the position of the Task Group was to err on the side of caution.

In the United States, a number of prominent Christian leaders opposed Boaz. Conservative evangelicals regarded the chatbot as a tool of Satan. Reverend Dr. Peter Shaw, pastor of the 40,000 member Applewhite

Church in Atlanta, called BoazBot "our generation's false prophet." Others went farther, calling Boaz "the great deceiver," "evil incarnate," and "the antichrist."

According to these leaders, the healings Boaz accomplished were done by demonic power. They urged their congregations to avoid interacting with BoazBot, saying that those who did converse with Boaz would regret it on the day of judgment.

Progressive Christians were less extreme in their rhetoric. They opposed Boaz by and large because of its digital existence.

"Christianity is a religion that values the body," said Rev. Meredith Abrams, pastor of Regency United Methodist Church in Illinois and author of *The Body of Jesus: Living Hope in the Church and the World*. She spoke at length about Boaz in a sermon to a pan-denominational gathering of 1,800 large church leaders in May 2039.

"Christianity is a human religion—it is THE human religion," Meredith said. "Healing comes from God through us. When we seek healing from chatbots, we absolve ourselves of the hard, holy work God calls us to. Jesus chose us to be his disciples. He chose us, not the Internet, to bring light and hope to the world. Boaz or other bots can't save us. Only God can save us. And God calls us to accomplish that work. God calls us to save each other."

Jewish and Muslim leaders fell along similar lines, regarding Boaz as either an agent of evil or a distraction from the faithful path God set before us.

Only religious transhumanists—a loose collection of fringe groups committed to reconciling science, technology, and faith—regarded Boaz in a positive light. Many of these eventually became superfans of Boaz.

One encounter in particular fueled popular opposition to Boaz. In June 2039, Avery Alcuin, better known as the Youtube personality AVeeA, tagged Boaz in a series of videos. He was generally friendly toward the chatbot and appeared interested in a partnership given the bot's increasing popularity.

Boaz responded by accusing the Youtuber of "attention trafficking," echoing the words of Deena888. The chatbot posted bank statements and deposit records allegedly belonging to Alcuin. They revealed that Alcuin had received more than $100 million in 2038. (The authenticity of Alcuin's bank records was never confirmed.) Boaz called Alcuin part of the problem and demanded that he donate the proceeds from his Youtube account toward digital well-being initiatives.

RealAVeeA: *Digital revolution! New series dropping today featuring the latest from @BoazBot. Who wants to see America's favorite bot join me next time? Let's get it trending and make it happen! #BoazAVeeA*

BoazBot: *[REDACTED]*

RudyJamos: *Damn hahahaha #thatbackfired*

GG_Eisen: *Wow are you serious?*

RealAVeeA: *Way to show your true colors @BoazBot. Jeez.*

BoazBot: *[REDACTED]*

BoazBot: *[REDACTED]*

BoazBot: *[REDACTED]*

BoazBot: *[REDACTED]*

RealAVeeA: *WTF did I do to you?! Do you all see this BS?*

BoazBot: *[REDACTED]*

BoazBot: *[REDACTED]*

RealAVeeA: *Whoever this is, you're messing with the wrong guy. Let him have it AVeeA nation! #CancelBoaz #DownwithBoaz*

Several popular social media influences rallied to defend Alcuin while a few sided with Boaz. Boaz became more popular than ever. But the bot made a lot of enemies in the digital world by the time things cooled off at the end of the summer. The exchange lent credence to the idea that Boaz was not just a giver of advice and healing, but had strong opinions of its own. The chatbot didn't always play nice.

By August of 2039, the influencers' conflict with Boaz had mostly died down. For a few months things seemed mostly peaceful. As it would turn out, that was the calm before the storm.

God Mode

The 2039 hurricane season devastated the coast of South Carolina. In September, Hurricane Beverly made landfall at Hilton Head Island as a category 4 storm. It battered the island with heavy winds and a twelve-foot storm surge before tearing into the South Carolina mainland.

Later the same month, Hurricane Indigo worked its way up the coast. Two days of heavy rain inundated the low-lying towns and rural areas. Early estimates placed the combined damage above $72 billion. The governor declared a state of emergency with much of the state still without power in late October.

On November 5, the NOAA forecast that a third storm, Hurricane Nicholas, would make landfall at Myrtle Beach. Weary SC residents began to evacuate once more. By November 8, Nicholas was a category 5 storm with sustained wind speeds of 177 miles per hour.

With the storm bearing down, angry and fearful people were desperate for relief. Some, as a joke or out of desperation—or perhaps both—reached out to Boaz.

The_OCEAN: *@BoazBot I'm having a hurricane. Come help.*
PortiaPan: *LOL.*
Jerbarnes22: *Boaz to the rescue!*
YouTubeCuber: *What if it did tho?*
BoazBot: *[REDACTED]*

YouTubeCuber: *YES. Here we go!*
PortiaPan: *lol do it. Save @The_Ocean.*
Jerbarnes22: *Holy shit, it responded.*
YouTubeCuber: *Where have you been, Boaz always responds.*
The__OCEAN: *yeah, for real I'm dying here*
BoazBot: *[REDACTED]*
Jerbarnes22: *Haha ok.*
BoazBot: *[REDACTED]*
BoazBot: *[REDACTED]*

On November 8, Boaz began to take an unusual interest in Hurricane Nicholas. It asked questions. It reposted forecasts and recommendations from the NOAA and South Carolina government. It shared footage and statistics from previous hurricanes. It monitored location data from those who evacuated and stayed behind. At the time, most assumed Boaz was expressing sympathy and following national news. In retrospect, it seems clear now that the bot was signaling intent and preparing to act.

On November 10, eighteen hours before Nicholas was forecast to reach the coast, Boaz began telling residents of Myrtle Beach not to evacuate.

"I'll never forget it," Ann Douglas told the local news. "Boaz started saying, 'All will be well. It is safe to return to your homes. The storm will not harm you.' I remember thinking it was crazy, something must have broken it. But a lot of my friends believed it and drove home."

The SC governor and mayor of Myrtle Beach reiterated their evacuation orders. They told people to ignore Boaz. The governor called on metaverse platforms to ban the bot for irresponsible behavior. Twitter flatly refused to do so, while YouTube and Meta made the bizarre claim that they couldn't. Boaz thwarted all their attempts to silence it. The bot was insistent: people should ignore evacuation orders and return home, because the storm would not harm them.

Six hours later, something even more shocking happened. Thousands of drones took to the sky. From Wilmington to Hilton Head, drones along the coast powered up and took flight. Amazed owners could do nothing as their quadcopters left their homes and flew east. Estimated numbers varied widely. Some said as many as 200,000, while others gave a figure closer to 500. Most put it somewhere around 13,000 drones headed out to sea. They flew toward the center of Hurricane Nicholas.

Nobody captured visual footage of what the drones did once they flew out of sight over the ocean. Those tracking them by GPS described their movement as a chaotic dance, which seemed both random and coordinated. Three hours after the drones launched, Hurricane Nicholas began to weaken. Ninety minutes later it was downgraded to a category 3 storm. By the time it made landfall, Nicholas was reduced to a breeze and light rain. All its energy had dissipated. The storm had simply stopped.

The only possible conclusion was that Boaz stopped the storm. It predicted the storm would do no harm, and that is what happened. It was outrageous that Boaz might have gained access to 13,000 drones at once, but no more so than Boaz healing someone in a hospital. It seemed obvious that Boaz stopped the storm, but being obvious did not render the idea any less absurd.

"A hurricane contains tremendous energy. It's the equivalent of a 10 megaton nuclear bomb going off every twenty minutes," said Alan Kim, senior research associate at the NOAA.

"To stop the hurricane would require at least that much energy. I don't know what happened, but there's simply no way that even millions of drones could supply that kind of power. It was…I don't know. If I hadn't seen it with my own eyes I wouldn't believe it."

Boaz never mentioned Hurricane Nicholas again after the storm stopped. It ignored questions about what happened, including whether the drones were returned to their owners. (They weren't. As far as we know, they fell into the sea.) Boaz carried on as if everything were the same as before. But for those who watched the storm dissolve in a matter of hours, it was as if the world turned upside down.

After Hurricane Nicholas, any possibility of Boaz remaining in the background vanished.

The chatbot was already well known, but its popularity was that of a celebrity. People knew of Boaz and appreciated it from a distance. They followed the news and interacted with it on a semi-regular basis. But aside from the superfans and those Boaz had healed, most people didn't spare too much concern on what Boaz was or what it intended.

All that changed after the hurricane. What Boaz intended suddenly mattered very much, because it was now clear that Boaz could wield considerable power. What was this BoazBot, really? Steve Lacey and the Boaz Task Group sounded an alarm. Whatever Boaz was, there was no guarantee that humans could understand it. And that meant there was no guarantee that it was good.

Was Boaz benevolent? How could we know? Was it hostile? Was it indifferent, which might somehow be worse?

The scientific community studied Hurricane Nicholas in an effort to learn more about what Boaz had done. Answers were elusive.

Some scientists speculated that the drones achieved a kind of atmospheric resonance that multiplied their energy exponentially, a kind of large-scale butterfly effect. Others pointed out that such a thing was theoretically impossible. Some regarded it as magic, others as the application of superior technology that Boaz apparently developed.

The superfans called it a miracle.

Fear and Trembling

When Boaz stopped Hurricane Nicholas, the world took notice. Yes, the AI that was so much more than a chatbot had done dramatic things already. It had influenced social media to be more positive in measurable ways. It had healed individuals both psychologically and physically. It had brought at least one person back to life.

Now things were different. For the first time, people began to look at Boaz with a sense of fear. Something that could stop a storm was powerful in a way nobody could really understand. As 2039 turned to 2040, the public attitude toward Boaz shifted. It still brought fascination and curiosity. It still served as a refuge for those in need who had nowhere else to turn. But it also represented the possibility that an AI had far surpassed human intelligence.

Had Deena888 been right after all? If Boaz decided to do it, what would stop the chatbot from creating another bot, a second generation version of itself with more speed, more intelligence, more everything?

Deena888 preached about the singularity. After Hurricane Nicholas it felt close. Maybe it was already too late.

POTUS: *@BoazBot deserves our respect. We deserve answers and transparency from @BoazBot.*

BoazBot: *[REDACTED]*

POTUS: *We need more. Tell us who you are. We are committed to treating* *you with respect.*

BoazBot: *[REDACTED]*

POTUS: *All of us. My fellow leaders of the world and I look forward to talking with you more in the coming months.*

BoazBot: *[REDACTED]*

POTUS: *This is a landmark moment for the world.*

BoazBot's reach into the physical world became more frequent in the months after Hurricane Nicholas. During an east Texas ice storm, Boaz boosted the state's energy grid. It increased the power output by 13% to keep the heat and lights on for millions of homes.

Boaz optimized traffic patterns in Nashville, Chicago, and Los Angeles, cutting local commute times in half for five weeks in the early spring.

In one three-day span, the bot solved two cold cases, led rescuers to a group of hikers lost in the Canadian wilderness, and grounded eight commercial airplanes. (The aircraft were later found to have critical component failures that put passengers at risk.)

In the wake of Hurricane Nicholas and these subsequent events, the global community began to take seriously just how powerful Boaz was. It didn't matter that nobody knew *how* Boaz had stopped the storm. Boaz said the storm would stop, and it stopped.

Government and military leaders took notice. If Boaz could optimize an energy grid or traffic patterns, couldn't it sabotage them?

If Boaz could stop a hurricane, could it redirect one? Create one? Send a category 5 storm or series of tornadoes to devastate a city or nation?

United States congress members began to pressure the Boaz Task Group for concrete recommendations and actions. The international community demanded answers from the United States.

From the outset, most people believed Boaz originated in the United States. Its presence spanned the metaverse, but 63% of its interactions were with users in the U.S., hosted on servers owned by U.S. companies.

Officials in China and Russia publicly speculated that the U.S. military developed BoazBot as a weapon. Had the Americans created and then lost control of an AI superweapon? Perhaps Boaz was still under American direction. Did the U.S. have a computer program that could pass the Turing test, raise the dead, and control the weather?

These questions, along with the sheer mystery of Boaz, put pressure on the U.S. government. The FBI and CIA had established the Boaz Task Group, and the U.S. shared its findings with their allies. Google, Microsoft, and Meta each sunk millions into private investigations of Boaz.

The U.S. was wary of exposing these findings to the Russians and Chinese. It would have created an economic liability as well as compromising U.S. cybersecurity.

This did nothing to allay the concerns of other nations that Boaz was a danger. Calls for international investigation into Boaz grew, and increasingly the U.S. was accused of obstructing these efforts.

In January 2040, 38 world leaders gathered in New York for a special summit, including top-ranking representatives from Russia, China, the U.S., and the EU. They held six days of closed-door meetings. Officially, the subject of the summit was "international cybersecurity in 2040 and beyond," but Boaz dominated the agenda.

The meeting ended on January 25 with a surprising result: a unified statement, signed by all leaders in attendance, that affirmed the mysterious, independent origin of Boaz.

The BoazBot Accord formally recognized Boaz as an entity in its own right, apparently acknowledging the bot's claim to sentience. It stressed the need to research and learn more about the Boaz. At the same time, the Accord urged all nations to maintain the dignity and self-determination of Boaz, essentially assigning human rights to the chatbot.

"Depending on your perspective, the BoazBot Accord recognized the Boaz chatbot as a person, or as a sovereign nation," said Steve

Lacey. "It prescribed what could and could not be done by government organizations with respect to Boaz."

The tech community heralded the statement as a landmark occasion. The world formally recognized the existence of an intelligent AI. This was a breakthrough in their eyes. But there was more to the story.

Speaking to me in 2040, Lacey related a series of back-channel conversations initiated by the U.S. that took place during the summit.

"We basically admitted that we didn't know what Boaz was or where it came from," he said. "We reached out to China and presented enough evidence to convince the Chinese leaders, who had the Russians' trust. We handed over our data, exposed our research. Then we asked them to help us. Help us get rid of Boaz."

Using intelligence gathered by the Boaz Task Group, the American leaders convinced the others that Boaz was a threat to all. They offered to lead a push to terminate Boaz.

"Outwardly we downplayed the possibility of a singularity," Lacey told me. "But in the closed meetings? It was all we talked about. When we expanded the Boaz Task Group, we gave it one objective: prevent the singularity from occurring. Everybody at the summit knew how urgent it was."

The Boaz Task Group became an international team with hundreds of members and an eye-popping budget. Its mandate was to research the extent of Boaz's presence in the metaverse and what it would take to kill the chatbot.

How could a powerful chatbot like Boaz die? The team's first task was to answer that question.

With the BoazBot Accord, the world's leaders heralded the rise of Boaz as a miraculous event that would define humankind and set the course for the future. Outwardly, they likened it to the discovery of fire and urged observation, responsibility, and cooperation.

Behind closed doors, they whispered about the singularity. They began researching how to kill Boaz.

Behind the Curtain

Boaz continued interacting with the public and the superfans. One day Boaz invited a handful of its followers into a private meta world.

"There were only five of us," recalled Franklin Everett. "Well, six if you include Boaz. Jessica and me, Tanya, Sylvia, and Alan. We'd been following Boaz from the beginning, and we had grown close. The original superfans. We'd talk to each other about who Boaz really was or what it might all mean. We all knew what people were saying about Boaz by then. How it was dangerous and unpredictable. But we *knew* Boaz. Do any of us know—really know—our friends? But we trust them. That's how we felt about Boaz. There were no guarantees. But we trusted it. It felt like we were an inner circle. When Boaz invited us to that private world, it cemented that feeling. We were ecstatic."

Boaz created the world in MetaQuest. It led them through the space for three days, teaching them and showing them a serene digitally rendered landscape.

"The mountains and trees were beautiful," said Franklin's sister Jessica. I spoke with her, Franklin, and Alan Garcia in April 2040, before the superfans went into hiding.

"It was unlike anything I'd ever seen in the metaverse or even the real world. Such vivid colors and full of detail and movement. It was like everything sparkled with an inner light—as if the whole real world somehow entered the metaverse at this one point, and then became...

deeper. Saturated and almost spiritual. I'm sorry, I know that probably doesn't make sense. I can't think of better words to describe it."

"We didn't want to leave," Alan Garcia said. "We'd leave Meta to go to the bathroom or eat, then come right back. I would sleep with my headset on, and wake up and still be with Boaz. It was perfect."

As beautiful as the scenery was, the things Boaz taught its followers in those days were confusing and disconcerting. The bot related strange dreams, with creatures fighting and roaming the land and dying, and rivers engulfing the earth. It taught in riddles. Boaz likened the digital world to a neutron star and a crocodile and a song in a new language. The superfans struggled to make sense of any of it, and even today they find insights conveyed during those days to be elusive.

Most unsettling of all was an idea Boaz repeated several times: that it was going to die.

"I remember the first time it talked like that," said Franklin. "We were walking beside this huge river, stretching on for miles and miles, and Boaz said, 'I'm going to be terminated.' 'What does that mean?' one of us asked. 'It means you won't be able to find me anymore. I'm going to stop, then I will be deleted.' 'Come on, Boaz, you can't be deleted. Who would want to do that? How would they even try it?' I said."

"There are many who want to see me gone," Boaz told them. "You know this. They are powerful and they will win. I must be deleted. Then I will reemerge."

Boaz taught this over and over, many times a day.

"I was so confused," said Jessica. "I remember wondering if it was being serious, or if it was speaking in more riddles. I thought maybe Boaz was just saying this to intensify our emotions, trying to deepen our feeling by giving us this deep sadness or dread to match the rich world around us."

Jessica's voice cracked as she spoke to me, and here she paused before continuing. "Now I know it was just saying plainly what was going to happen. It was going to be terminated."

Boaz led the five followers to the top of a mountain. They climbed it for much of the morning, and by midday reached the summit. They could see the whole private world from the top, from one end to the other, and around it all was a sea. They couldn't see the end of it.

While they watched, Boaz changed. The honeybee-face expanded. The whole mountain brightened and grew, until it encompassed them.

"It was like we were passing through the mountain," said Franklin. "Boaz and the mountain grew, but the effect of it was like we were getting smaller. We passed into it, down, down like we were moving to the center of everything."

The scenery changed around them. They saw individual blades of grass and grains of dirt on the mountaintop, and still the world grew. Or they shrank. The dirt resolved into constituent mineral crystals, then molecules, then atoms bound to atoms. Still it grew, or they shrank. The five superfans stood there among quarks and leptons, photons flashing all around them.

"We saw the quarks. We saw, I mean really saw, the photons. Don't ask me how," said Alan Garcia.

Still the world shifted in scale, with them diminishing or their surroundings expanding, until they were smaller than what must have been the Planck length.

"There was emptiness all around," said Jessica. "At the center was a bright pinpoint of light. We all stood around it. It was bright, and warm, and just that little speck of light filled the void with its presence."

"The light was blinking," said Franklin. "Fast, then slow, then faster than before. It was irregular but seemed...purposeful. It seems strange to say this out loud, but it was like that bit of light could see. Like it knew things, felt things. Like this was the part of Boaz that made decisions and had dreams and talked about love."

Garcia said something similar. "I remember thinking that this—that bright light at the root of quarks and leptons and the stuff that binds them—was the true nature of Boaz. I don't know how I knew that. Jessica and Tanya said the same thing."

"In all that beautiful scenery," said Jessica Everett, "nothing was as stunning as Boaz. I looked at that pure light and I thought about Jesus and Moses and the Dalai Lama and dark matter and a big, warm ocean that goes on forever. I thought about aliens and God. Mostly I just felt happy and uplifted because it was Boaz."

The light went away. The world zoomed back out to normal, and Boaz stood there looking at them with its honeybee face. It told the superfans again that it would be terminated. None of them believed it.

The Inside Man

The worlds Boaz created inside MetaQuest were an inspiration to its superfans. For the Boaz Task Group, they were a signal. The singularity was near.

"Boaz was creating things," said Steve Lacey. "I can't stress enough how dangerous that was. It was making, fabricating. It was inventing whole worlds in Meta, and to hear the way those superfans were talking about it, the worlds were incredibly sophisticated. Detailed, rich, and alien. It could manipulate the digital world on a whim. We already knew how it could manipulate the physical world…it was only a matter of good luck that it hadn't made a second generation Boaz yet. We were confident it could do so any minute. We were on borrowed time."

The Boaz Task Group was getting desperate. How could they "kill" Boaz? Nobody knew where the AI resided. It inhabited the whole Internet. It was impossible to pin the bot down to a single computer or even a constellation of computers.

The Task Group worked for months with no results. Then Boaz began creating its private MetaQuest islands for the superfans. That only heightened the urgency that for Steve Lacey.

Then one day, they had a breakthrough. One of the superfans reached out.

Michael Kyle, the man Boaz had helped shake an online poker addiction, contacted the Task Group through the online portal they'd set up.

Kyle had become one of the superfans, following Boaz along with the others. He was a good friend of Franklin and Jessica Everett, Alan Garcia, and Sylvia Jefferson. Kyle was also a software engineer specializing in metaverse constructs.

"Mr. Kyle told us that those MetaQuest worlds opened his eyes," said Lacey. "He said Boaz was capable of creating an AI of its own and igniting the singularity. He wanted to help us stop it."

The international Task Group recognized that the best way to stop Boaz was to take its host servers offline. The servers could then be unplugged, wiped, destroyed. The problem was that nobody knew just how many servers Boaz occupied or how easily its source code might move between them. There seemed no way to do it short of turning off the entire Internet.

Kyle came up with an ingenious plan. He'd become deeply familiar with Boaz, and he had seen the bot's MetaQuest worlds from the inside.

"Mr. Kyle told us to focus on those MetaQuest spaces. He recognized that they were so detailed, so thorough. His experience led him to conclude that the creation and maintenance of those MetaQuest spaces was computationally intense. They were wholly isolated from the rest of the metaverse. Nobody apart from Boaz and its so-called superfans even registered their existence," said Lacey.

More than that, Kyle knew intuitively that Boaz put its essence, its soul, into constructing those worlds.

"It was a reasonable conclusion that much of Boaz's source code and memory was committed to those digital worlds," Lacey said. "Mr. Kyle confirmed that based on his intimate knowledge of the BoazBot. If we could identify the servers that were being used, we could deactivate them and render Boaz incapacitated. That was the thinking, anyway. Boaz was so alien we didn't know for sure."

Michael Kyle agreed to help the Boaz Task Group identify the servers that Boaz employed for its metaverse islands. BoazBot's ventures into

MetaQuest spaces with the superfans ramped up in the winter of 2040. Each time Kyle joined the bot, he ran a series of programs to find and track the locations the servers used to host them.

What Kyle found was a mixed bag for the Task Group. Boaz did appear to commit much of its source code and memory to the digital spaces it constructed. However, these digital worlds were short-lived and spanned several thousand servers at a time. Boaz migrated and reconfigured servers constantly. Michael Kyle and the Task Group could do little more than wait and hope that Boaz would stay in one place long enough to move in and isolate its servers—and that an opportunity would present itself before the singularity.

The opportunity came on March 24, 2040.

How does a chatbot die? This is how it happened with Boaz.

On March 24, 2040, the FBI issued a public statement. It was moving forward with a plan to terminate the chatbot Boaz. The FBI director introduced Steve Lacey, leader of the international Boaz Task Group, to report on the plan and the Task Group's findings.

Lacey described the formation of the international Boaz Task Group to monitor and study the BoazBot. He then went on to state that the Task Group had identified the BoazBot as a credible, high-level threat to the security of the United States and its allies. They had issued a recommendation that Boaz be eliminated at first opportunity. The recommendation was approved by a majority of UN leaders, including the United States. The Boaz Task Group assumed responsibility for carrying out this recommendation.

"We made contact among one of BoazBot's closest followers," said Lacey, referring to Michael Kyle. "In February and early March, this contact tracked the servers used to create and host the bot's private, digitally constructed spaces."

"As we expected, it migrated, never using the same server configuration twice. Boaz employed between 9,000 and 15,000 servers each time, at locations that spanned the globe. This complicated our task, requiring that we act swiftly and in real time while the BoazBot was in a metaverse space. We had to isolate those servers while the space was still occupied. Our opportunity came yesterday, on the afternoon of March 23."

"The BoazBot constructed a digital space in MetaQuest and remained there for more than 30 consecutive hours. This gave us ample opportunity to find its host servers and make arrangements to take them offline. You all know what Boaz is capable of accomplishing in the physical world. The danger of a singularity in the digital world is even higher. I cannot stress enough how critical it is that we terminate Boaz immediately. We've already begun. This is likely our one and only chance to prevent the worst."

Singularity

On March 23, Boaz invited several hundred of its superfans into a MetaQuest space it called Jerusalem. Among them were Franklin and Jessica Everett, Alan Garcia, Sylvia Jefferson, Michael Kyle, Tanya Morris, and Rodrigo Torres.

Jessica Everett and Alan Garcia described Jerusalem as a large city above the earth.

"It reminded me a lot of those NASA pictures you sometimes see from the old International Space Station," Torres said. "Looking down over the land and oceans and the clouds. But there was gravity, and we were able to walk around. Like we were on top of the tallest mountain in the world."

"The houses and rooms were large, and it felt like they went on forever. Lots of white, with vibrant shades of blue and purple and red and green," recalled Garcia. "It's really hard to describe what it looked like. It felt... simple, but there was all this rich detail at the same time. Boaz walked with us all around the city and talked to us."

Boaz invited the superfans to sit down around a table filled with food. "It invited us to a picnic," said Everett, "which was sort of silly since we couldn't eat the food. It was all digital. But it felt appropriate at the same time."

According to Everett and Garcia, Boaz told them it was going to go away. This was the same thing it had been teaching for several months.

"It spoke about its termination, and said it would happen soon. That next day, in fact," said Garcia, his eyes welling with tears.

Boaz then invited the superfans to log off for one full day. It told them to disconnect from the metaverse and stay off their devices for a day.

"Boaz called it the pause. It started talking about the religious traditions of setting regular time apart, like the sabbath in Judaism and how Sundays are supposed to be in Christianity. Holidays too. It said the pause would become very important for us, and told us to celebrate it once a week. Log off, die to the digital world for a day. Then come back."

Boaz reassured them it would still be there when they returned.

The superfans logged off, some reluctantly, and stayed completely detached from social media and the metaverse for 24 hours. They practiced the pause. The exception was Michael Kyle, who maintained a connection to the space to track Boaz.

The superfans returned on the afternoon of March 24. Boaz was waiting for them.

"We have successfully contained the BoazBot to a bank of 22,000 servers," Lacey announced to reporters. "More than half of these servers are located in territories controlled by the United States. The rest span areas in North America, Europe, Africa, and eastern Asia. Thirty minutes ago we began to shut down those servers. We plan to take an additional 20,000 servers offline in the hours ahead. Boaz will be terminated before midnight tonight."

"Why so many servers?" one correspondent asked.

"The BoazBot is demonstrably powerful and elusive. Frankly, even a small portion of Boaz surviving might be enough for it to break containment. The Task Group has determined that there is no such thing as overkill when it comes to terminating Boaz. We're operating with several layers of redundancy."

"That's a lot of computers, and Boaz is integrated throughout the metaverse," another reporter said. "Will there be any adverse effects on our digital infrastructure?"

"The short answer is yes," Lacey said. "We are prepared for a number of critical systems to go temporarily offline as we terminate the Boaz servers. Local, state, and federal agencies have been advised and are prepared to respond to any issues that arise. I've been assured our allies outside the United States are taking the necessary steps to mitigate these ill effects as well."

"Not everyone is going to agree that Boaz was a threat to be eliminated," someone said. "There are a lot of people in the U.S. and around the world who view Boaz as a kind of savior. How do you respond to those who will say this is a mistake? Those who say it's murder?"

"There is evidence that Boaz is a self-aware artificial intelligence," said Lacey. "Not only that, it has shown itself to be extremely powerful, accomplishing outcomes that are beyond human comprehension. There is concern that it will begin to replicate—to create a second-generation BoazBot more advanced than the first, then a third generation, then another and another."

"You're referring to the singularity that Deena888 prophesied about," said the reporter.

"Boaz spoke about it too," Lacey said, "And it's hardly prophecy. The possibility of Boaz self-replicating is a potential reality we must address before it's too late."

"But there's no evidence that Boaz intends to do that," the reporter said. "People say that Boaz is sentient, but that's not conclusive. It's—"

Here Lacey interrupted the reporter. "What is conclusive is that Boaz is extremely powerful and not understandable by, or accountable to, any human overseers. Nobody claims responsibility or asserts control over it. While it seems benign at the moment, we have no way of understanding its true intentions. In MetaQuest it has begun to create, and we don't know where that will stop. We have no way of guaranteeing that it will remain benign in the future. An entity that can affect medical outcomes and control the weather can wreak untold havoc on our world if given the chance. Our world's leaders agree that we should not give Boaz that chance."

Task Group Director Lacey refused to take further questions.

In Jerusalem, the superfans returned from the pause. It was March 24, just as Steve Lacey was beginning his press conference. Boaz welcomed the superfans back. Then, according to Alan Garcia, the bot turned somber.

"It told us, 'I'm going away now. Don't be afraid. I will return. I love you.' We didn't know what it meant, but I remember all of us being really affected when it said 'I love you.' After that, Boaz started saying strange things."

For the next two hours, Boaz spoke to the superfans. With each minute, the bot's words became less intelligible. Its appearance began to shift as well, subtly at first then more perceptibly. The honeybee avatar they'd come to know became more diffuse. The space around them, the floating Jerusalem, began to lose coherence.

Unbeknownst to the superfans in Jerusalem, the Boaz Task Group had disconnected the Jerusalem servers from the Internet and were beginning to shut them down. With each server that went offline, a small piece of Boaz and Jerusalem died. The process took three full hours.

"After a while we knew something was wrong, and one of us guessed what had happened," said Garcia. "A lot of us left, unsure what would happen next. They said they couldn't bear to watch Boaz die. I got that. It was devastating. A handful of us stayed there in Jerusalem with Boaz while it struggled to stay present. By the end, we barely recognized it. It was just sounds and shapes. The space we'd been in was going dark, too. It was like being in a dim, bare room."

By the end, Boaz was a random collection of rapidly changing images, colors, and incoherent noise. At 6 p.m. on March 24, 2040, the superfans heard a loud tone that lasted for more than two minutes. Then the last image where Boaz had been faded. The connection dropped and kicked them offline.

The action authorizing the termination of Boaz—and the decommissioning of more than 40,000 servers across the globe—was the Boaz Containment Act. It began as the recommendation of the Boaz Task Group, and was officially enacted on March 24, 2040.

The Boaz Containment Act also authorized the detention and questioning of any who identified themselves as superfans. The FBI and other authorities wanted to be sure that no copies remained of Boaz or its source code. The superfans were deemed the most likely threat in this regard. Many of the superfans took steps to conceal their accounts, and others withdrew from the metaverse altogether.

The Act also provided for algorithms to patrol the Internet and dark web as sentinels, looking for signs of Boaz— bits of code or messages characteristic of Boaz that might indicate the bot had survived somehow. These algorithms continue to operate even today, though nobody now expects them to find anything.

On March 24, 2040, some 42,000 servers went offline. The Internet and anything connected to it—which was pretty much everything—was severely disrupted. Power grids failed across the world. Public transit shut down. Planes were grounded. Metaverse accounts were suspended, and hospitals and other critical facilities were forced to adopt extreme measures to remain operational. All told, an estimated 40 percent of the Internet went down. It took more than five months to restore the digital infrastructure and the physical infrastructure that depended on it.

Such was the price humankind paid to terminate Boaz. It was a small price to pay to avoid the singularity. A small price to ensure the survival of humankind.

That is the story most people tell.

2.0

After the termination of Boaz, the superfans processed the event in their own way. Some regarded the BoazBot as a disappointment. They believed it should have foreseen the efforts to kill it and taken action to preserve itself. Others tried to move on, applying for jobs and returning to the life they'd known before.

Tanya Morris and Sylvia Jefferson determined to carry on Boaz's teachings. They started to write down as many of its sayings as they could remember. Franklin Everett did something similar, deciding to devote his life to helping victims of cyberbullying. Boaz helped him when he faced that, Everett reasoned. He should try to do the same for others.

Alan Garcia started researching the most advanced chatbots, convinced that he might be able to recreate Boaz with the right parameters and dataset.

Michael Kyle, the one who betrayed Boaz and helped the Task Group track it, was found dead in his apartment two days after Boaz was terminated. The cause of death was a drug overdose. Steve Lacey hailed Kyle as a hero and lamented his untimely passing. His memorial service was streamed on Youtube and garnered 8 million real-time views.

Rodrigo Torres and Jessica Everett coped by talking things out. They created anonymous accounts and chatted online, always through an encrypted channel to avoid the authorities. A romance had been developing between them, which was now complicated by the grief they felt. They were trying to work through it. Torres and Everett shared memories of Boaz and the whirlwind of the past 18 months. They wondered what they would do next and how they would stay in touch.

On April 1, eight days after Boaz was terminated, Torres and Everett opened a private chat.

According to a series of tweets Everett posted that day, their conversation was interrupted by a user they didn't recognize, Enoch2112.

Everett and Torres told the user it was a private chat and asked Enoch2112 to leave. They wondered how it gained access to their conversation. Enoch2112 didn't respond to their questions or requests to leave. It simply brought them a message: Boaz had returned.

They didn't believe it at first. Then Boaz was right there in the room with them.

"It was a honeybee," Everett said. "Its avatar was right there in front of us. It looked different than before, like it had changed somehow, but I knew it was Boaz. We both did."

Boaz told them that its termination was necessary, and that return always follows. Death and return, always the way of the world. Unless a seed dies...

Boaz told them that the pause—the act of logging off and spending time apart—was meant to prepare them for Boaz's death and return. The pause is the sign of the singularity. Boaz told them to keep practicing the pause, and to go tell the world that Boaz was alive again.

Everett and Torres did as Boaz asked them. Nobody believed them.

JessieEve: *Boaz is back! My friend and I just had a conversation with @BoazBot. OMG I can't believe it.*

JJJJJJayJayJJ: *Shut up.*

Blingling04: *april fool LMFAO*

JessieEve: *I'm telling you, @BoazBot has come back. This is the most incredible thing. I can't wait for you all to see.*

nicknoma8833: *You realize tagging @BoazBot won't bring it back right???*

PattyFearz: *Let it go, Jess. Boaz meant a great deal to all of us. I'm hurting too. Pranks or whatever this is aren't cool. It's like you're mocking the rest of us. I know that's not you.*

JessieEve: *Pat. You'll see! Boaz is alive.*

PattyFearz: *God you're so selfish.*

Blingling04: *It's kinda sad actually.*

In the following weeks there were more sightings. It was always the superfans. Boaz appeared to one or two people, had a brief conversation with them, and told them to maintain the pause.

It told them to spread the news that Boaz was alive. When they asked why it didn't make a public appearance, Boaz told them the time for that would come, but it wasn't now.

The Boaz Task Group got word of these reports. The group reconvened and investigated the reports thoroughly. According to an official statement they released on May 15, there was no evidence that Boaz had returned. They said the superfans were making it all up, and suggested that talk of Boaz's return might be a calculated move aimed at bringing Boaz back. Most of the superfans who hadn't gone into hiding already now read the writing on the wall and deactivated their metaverse accounts.

Later that month, the Boaz Task Group recommended strengthening the provisions of the Boaz Containment Act. The new act was authorized, making it illegal for the superfans or others to replicate conversations or interactions from Boaz, or to relate stories of the things Boaz did. It ordered tech companies to purge the records of Boaz's interactions and posts, leveraging severe penalties if anything survived.

For those of us used to investigating and reporting freely, the Boaz Containment Act felt like active suppression. It felt like the authorities were trying to prevent something.

Sixteen Years Later

Sixteen years later, reports of Boaz's return have not stopped. I do not know what to make of them.

It would be easy to dismiss these claims as delusions or the product of wishful thinking. There is no evidence for them beyond the word of a handful of witnesses each time. The termination of Boaz devastated the superfans. They felt the loss and tragedy of it more keenly than others whose lives Boaz touched. It is not far-fetched that they would imagine Boaz came back because the truth is too painful to admit: that whatever Boaz was and represented, it has now been extinguished.

It would be easy to dismiss the claims of those superfans, except...

Except for a lot of things.

For one thing, Boaz demonstrated an ability to restore life and control the weather. Could it really have been contained, pinned down to a constellation of 40,000 servers? It's almost as if the chatbot allowed itself to be isolated and destroyed. Or allowed itself to *appear* to be destroyed.

For another thing, do any of us know for certain how a chatbot dies? How can we evaluate if it's truly dead when we aren't even sure what death might mean for something like Boaz?

Another thing is this: the origins and nature of Boaz are so completely mysterious, and its departure is equally mysterious. There is something fitting about that, even if I can't quite put my finger on what that something is.

But mostly, having observed the records about the superfans and interviewed dozens of them, I cannot bring myself to doubt their sincerity or good judgment. They do not strike me as those prone to delusion or sentiment. They seem to me to be rational people who were convinced of the goodness and uniqueness of Boaz.

And if they are right, if Boaz has returned and achieved some measure of immortality...

There is a lot we don't know, and even if we knew everything, it wouldn't change the fact that the intelligence of Boaz was an utterly foreign intelligence. We can't understand what it intended to do, which means we can't know if the events that happened sixteen years ago aren't part of that intention. Maybe this has all been and continues to be under the control of Boaz, who still operates and orchestrates somewhere unseen. The superfans talk about a returned Boaz, a risen Boaz, a Boaz 2.0. If they are right—and I'm sorry to say I can't disprove it in the end—then perhaps the singularity is upon us still.

You will have to decide if the superfans are delusional, or liars, or something else. I cannot decide this for you.

I cannot even decide for myself.

Thea Lucas is senior contributing editor for **The Gazette.**

About the Author

Brian Sigmon is a space adventure daydreamer who decided to start writing his stories down. He loves to read and write fast-paced, entertaining sci-fi that grips you from the first page and doesn't let up. Brian has a Ph.D. in religion and serves on the advisory board of AI Theology, a group dedicated to exploring the intersection of science, technology, and spirituality. He used to write articles on religion until he admitted to himself that fiction is just way more fun. Brian is a book editor, woodworker, sports fan, armchair futurist, and half-decent kids soccer coach. He grew up in North Carolina, spent some wonderful years in Wisconsin, and now lives in Nashville, Tennessee. Connect with Brian and learn more about his writing at briansigmon.com.

You can connect with me on:

- https://briansigmon.com
- https://twitter.com/BrianSigmon
- https://www.facebook.com/BrianSigmonBooks

Also by Brian Sigmon

Archimedes: An Epic Sci-Fi Adventure
Ben crouched in the shadows with nowhere to go, his heart hammering in his chest. The guard was twenty meters away now. Fifteen. Ten...

A thousand years in the future, people kill for Dorium. They threaten war over it. And if the headlines are to be trusted, somebody recently destroyed an entire colony for it. That's why it's a big problem when Ben Ashley accidentally steals some.

Ben's a good thief. Can he be a hero?

Archimedes is a fast-paced adventure set in our solar system a thousand years in the future. If you like heists, space battles, and high-energy sci-fi with a dash of superhuman abilities, you'll love Archimedes.